Strega Nona's Magic Ring

Story and Pictures by

TOMIE dePAOLA

Simon & Schuster
Books for Young Readers
New York London Toronto Sydney New Delhi

For Paola Risposio,
who introduced me to Bambolona

SIMON & SCHUSTER BOOKS FOR YOUNG READERS
An imprint of Simon & Schuster Children's Publishing Division
1230 Avenue of the Americas, New York, New York 10020
Copyright © 1979 by Tomie dePaola
Originally published as *Big Anthony and the Magic Ring*
For information about special discounts for bulk purchases, please contact
Simon & Schuster Special Sales at 1-866-506-1949 or business@simonandschuster.com.
The Simon & Schuster Speakers Bureau can bring authors to your live event.
For more information or to book an event, contact the Simon & Schuster Speakers Bureau
at 1-866-248-3049 or visit our website at www.simonspeakers.com.
Book design by Laurent Linn
The text for this book was set in ITC Esprit Std.
The illustrations for this book were rendered in Prismacolor pencils, colored inks, and watercolor paints.
With appreciation and thanks to the Kerlan Collection, Children's Literature Research Collections,
University of Minnesota Libraries, for use of Tomie dePaola's original *Big Anthony and the Magic Ring* artwork.
Manufactured in China
0118 SCP
First Simon & Schuster Books for Young Readers hardcover edition March 2018
2 4 6 8 10 9 7 5 3 1
Library of Congress Cataloging-in-Publication Data
Names: DePaola, Tomie, 1934– author illustrator.
Title: Strega Nona's magic ring / story and pictures by Tomie dePaola.
Other titles: Big Anthony and the magic ring
Description: First edition. | New York : Simon & Schuster Books for Young Readers, [2018] |
Summary: When Big Anthony borrows Strega Nona's magic ring
to turn himself into a handsome man, he gets more trouble than fun.
Identifiers: LCCN 2016039499| ISBN 9781481477611 (hardcover) | ISBN 9781481477628 (ebook)
Subjects: | CYAC: Magic—Fiction. | Beauty, Personal—Fiction. | Witches—Fiction.
Classification: LCC PZ7.D439 Stf 2018 | DDC [E]—dc23 LC record available at https://lccn.loc.gov/2016039499

Wintertime was very quiet in the little town in Calabria where Strega Nona (Grandma Witch) and her helper Big Anthony lived. People came to Strega Nona to help them solve their troubles. Big Anthony did his chores and tried to behave himself. And every morning Bambolona, the baker's daughter, came to deliver the bread.

One day the sun began to shine a little brighter, the birds began to sing a little sweeter, and the flowers began to bloom everywhere. Spring had come, and Big Anthony began to drag his feet.

"Anthony," said Strega Nona, "whatever is the matter? You're sleeping late. Your chores are half done, and every time I look at you, you're gazing into space and sighing."

"Oh, Strega Nona, I don't know what's wrong with me," said Big Anthony. "Everything in my head is fuzzy."

"I think you have spring fever," said Strega Nona. "What you need is a little Night Life. Why don't you go to the village dance tonight? It would perk you up."

Big Anthony sighed again. "The village seems so far away," he said. "And anyway, who would dance with *me*?"

"Bambolona, the baker's daughter, would," said Strega Nona. "Why don't you ask her when she brings the bread?"

"Who?" asked Big Anthony (for in truth he had never noticed her).

When supper was finished and Strega Nona was straightening up her cupboard, she suddenly stopped and said to herself, "Ummm. A little Night Life. That's not a bad idea. It's been quite a while since *I* went to the village and danced the tarantella."

Then she began to bang the little drawers open and shut, looking into each of them.

The noise startled Big Anthony, who was sitting just outside gazing at the moon.

"What is Strega Nona doing?" he asked himself, peeking through a crack in the door.

"Aha, here it is," said Strega Nona, holding up a tiny golden ring. "I haven't used this in years."

She slipped the ring on the first finger of her right hand and then began to sing:

"O little band, my golden ring,
listen to the song I sing.
Make me look as I do not,
and to the village dance I'll trot."

There was a puff of smoke, and instead of Strega Nona, there stood a beautiful lady, in elegant clothes!

Big Anthony could hardly believe his eyes.

Secretly, Big Anthony followed the beautiful lady
all the way to the village square . . .

and there he watched her dance the tarantella all
night long.

When the dance was over, Big Anthony followed her back to Strega Nona's house.

There the lady sang:

"O shiny band, my golden ring,
again the little song I sing.
The dance is done,
the moon does wane.
Turn me back to me again."

Then she slipped the ring off her finger.

With a puff of smoke, there was Strega Nona!

"Oh," whispered Big Anthony, "if only I could get that ring. I would be the handsomest man in all of Calabria, and all the village ladies would want to dance with me."

Big Anthony decided to wait for his chance—which came the very next morning, after Bambolona brought the bread.

"Anthony, I must go and visit my godchildren," said Strega Nona, "now that it's Eastertide. Be a good *ragazzo*, stay out of trouble, do your chores, and don't drag your feet."

"*Sì*, yes, Strega Nona," said Big Anthony.

Round and round they went, dancing the tarantella.

So this is a little Night Life, thought Handsome Big Anthony happily.

After several hours Handsome Big Anthony was beginning
to get a little tired, but the ladies wouldn't let him stop dancing.

"*Caro*," they cried, "dance with me! Me, *caro*, next!" and
they began to push and shove.

They pushed and shoved so much that at last Handsome
Big Anthony got scared.

"*Un momento*—just a minute! Let me catch my breath,"
he cried.

But the pushing and shoving and grabbing and kissing
only went on more. Handsome Big Anthony began to run.
The ladies began to run too. After him.

Handsome Big Anthony stopped and sang:

"O shiny band, my golden ring,
again the little song I sing.
The dance is done, the moon does wane.
Turn me back to me again. *Please.*"

Then he tried to take off the ring, but it stuck fast.
"Mamma mia," he cried. "What am I going to do?"

Past the fountain, past the priest, past the sisters of the convent on their way to prayers he ran. . . .

Out through the gate—past the goats—into the countryside.
"Me! Me! Dance with me! *Amore!*" cried the ladies, close behind.

Handsome Big Anthony continued to run.

Again he sang the song, although he was out of breath.

Again he tugged at the ring. But it wouldn't budge.

At last, he climbed a cypress tree. Up to the very top.

Now he had nowhere to go.

"Help! Save me! Help!" he cried. And he sang some more and tugged some more. But it did no good.

The ladies reached the tree and shook it hard. Shook and shook and shook it.

"Come down, you handsome devil, you! Dance with us some more. With Maria! Concetta! Clorinda! Rosanna! Theresa! Francesca! Clotilda!" they cried.

Finally they shook the tree so hard that Handsome Big Anthony lost his grip and flew into the air.

"Oh no!" he cried. "Now they'll get me for sure!"

He landed on his handsome big nose right in front of
a little house—Strega Nona's house.

And Strega Nona was home from her visit.

It didn't take her the time to blow three kisses to see
what had happened.

"Anthony," she said, "where did you get my magic ring?"

"Oh, Strega Nona, help me, please. I only wanted a little fun. Just a little Night Life. I sang the song, but the ring is stuck. What am I to do? Here they come—they're after me! Please, make me *me* again."

Strega Nona opened a flagon of olive oil and rubbed some on his finger.

"Now," she said, "SING!"

Handsome Big Anthony loudly sang:

"O shiny band, my golden ring,
again the little song I sing.
The dance is done, the moon does wane.
Turn me back to me again."

The ring slipped off his finger, and when the puff
of smoke had cleared, there sat . . . plain Big Anthony.

"Where is he? Oh, where did he go? Where is that handsome devil?" cried the ladies from the village.

"There's no one here as you can see but me and Big Anthony," said Strega Nona.

Calling "Wait, wait, wait for us," the ladies rushed away. And soon they were out of sight.

"Oh, Anthony," said Strega Nona. "You will never learn!"

"Strega Nona, you saved my life. Never again, I promise—
never will I touch your magic," cried Big Anthony.

"Never mind, Big Anthony," said Strega Nona with a smile.
"There are other kinds of magic in the spring."